His Twisted Tail

A Paranormal Dating Agency Story

Melanie James

His Twisted Tail

A Paranormal Dating Agnecy Story

Copyright 2017 Melanie James

Published by MT Worlds Press, Inc.

Winter Springs, FL 32708

http://mtworldspress.com

Formatting by Celtic Formatting

All rights reserved under the International and Pan-American Copyright Conventions. No part of this book may be reproduced or transmitted in any form or by any means, electronic or mechanical, including photocopying, recording, or by any information storage and retrieval system, without permission in writing from the publisher.

This is a work of fiction. Names, places, characters and incidents are either the product of the author's imagination or are used fictitiously, and any resemblance to any actual persons, living or dead, organizations, events or locales is entirely coincidental.

http://mtworldspress.com

Acknowledgements

To the women in my life who always have my back—thank you. You mean more to me than you could ever possibly imagine!

Dedication

To my alpha male—love you.

One

The bright sun hung high in the sky, beating down on Calder Lorenson as he hammered away at another dilapidated roof. Lifting his head, he looked around and thought for the hundredth time that he was in way the hell over his head.

"You're the one who said yes to becoming the Alpha of Twisted Tail and taking over the pack. We could have easily walked away and started a new life somewhere other than this fixer-upper," his wolf reminded him for the umpteenth time.

"I know, but this place feels right. Like we're supposed to be here. The people here need me,

need us. Not only that, Gus asked us to take over here."

Gus Ecklund had been his mentor for many years. He looked up to the older man and respected his opinion. When Gus had explained the horrors the people at Twisted Tail had suffered under their old Alpha, Griffin Engle, Calder knew he had to step in and help those who needed it.

He had never expected to be Alpha of any pack. As the youngest of three sons born to an Alpha, Calder's place in the line of succession had been sealed until Gus had stepped in.

His mentor had sensed his wolf's powers and had worked to develop and grow them over the years they'd spent together. It was almost as if Gus knew that one day Calder would take over as Alpha at Twisted Tail.

Being the Alpha of Twisted Tail had sounded great, and he had already experienced some of the challenges he'd known were sure to come with the job. He never expected the transition to be a walk in the park, but sweet Jeebus—he had not expected every house, apartment complex, and building on pack territory to be in a state of total disrepair.

Everything needed something, people and buildings alike. As soon as he fixed one issue, five more seemed to spring up. It had been nonstop since the moment he'd arrived at Twisted Tail.

"How are you doing over there, Alex?" Calder asked, glancing over to the man working beside him.

Alex had approached him when he'd first set about with his plans to tackle the housing issues at Twisted Tail. Calder had been skeptical at first about Alex's intentions, but soon dismissed any worries he'd had about the man. He found that Alex truly wanted to help make his town and his pack better.

"Not too bad. It's nice to see someone take the initiative to clean this place up, even if you are an outsider."

Calder chugged his bottle of water thinking about what Alex had said. It had definitely been a point of contention with some members in the pack. They despised outsiders and wanted nothing more than for him to walk away. "I'm never going to live that down. Am I?"

"I'm just giving you a hard time. It's not a problem for me. I'm more interested in doing what's right for the whole pack, not just a few of the trouble makers. If this pack is going to survive it has to change. And the way I see it, the change you've brought has been positive. It's good for the pack and everyone in it. Those who have a problem with it are the holdouts from Griffin's reign of terror."

Calder nodded. "I figured as much."

And he had.

One of his strengths was the ability to read people. The ability to see who a person really was, what was in their heart and soul, made his job easier at times. It also led to disappointment in people more times than he cared to count. Over the years, he'd hesitated using his gift, feeling as if it were some sort of intrusion. He'd often think, 'who meets someone and immediately looks at their soul'? His gift was too intrusive and Calder didn't want to be that untrusting person. Life, with all of its grand betrayals, taught him to be that person.

He knew that his eyes darkened to a pitch black. He likened it to a second sight—one that gave him a glimpse of one's soul.

He had once believed in giving humans and shifters the benefit of the doubt, but being able to see when a person's soul had been possessed by pure evil had saved his life time and again. The special sight, as he liked to call it, had never let him down.

Not once.

Calder had taken advantage of his insight to catch that special glimpse of most of the pack members at Twisted Tail over the few short weeks since he had become Alpha. There was no question in his mind who he needed to watch his ass around, and those who would have his back when shit hit the fan.

Alex had his back. As one of the first members of the pack to offer his hand at helping to rebuild the community, he'd earned Calder's trust when it came to doing what was right for the pack. He worked his ass off and never once offered a single complaint.

Calder had heard stories about the suffering most of the pack had been forced to endure. The tales' survivors told about the atrocities the former Alpha had committed against his own pack—from starving his people to forced matings, brutal beatings, and public executions—made him and his wolf sick. Calder would make damn sure life at Twisted Tail changed for the better.

Signs of the frequent abuses were all around him. But he saw more than a beaten-down pack. He saw people, a pack, a town, desperately wanting a shot at a normal life, one that was free of the never-ending pain and humiliation that had been forced upon them. He saw a pack waiting for someone who cared enough about them to make change happen.

And change was what it was all about: getting the small community back on its feet again and fixing everything that had been broken, buildings and people alike.

He had to be that person. The person to offer strength and hope—a better life for all.

"I wanted to give you a heads up. I don't think those wanting to see you gone are going to come at you head on." Alex pulled his t-shirt off and used it to wipe his sweaty brow.

"What do you mean?" Calder asked in confusion. Wolves were nothing if not vicious when it came to defending their territory. The most direct route to challenge an Alpha would be initiating a fight. Everyone knew that—or so he thought. It made wonder what fresh hell awaited over the horizon.

"There's been whispers about having people search through all of the formal written pack law. I guess they're looking for a law that could make it illegal for you to continue on as Alpha. That way they could force you out without challenging you."

"Huh. I'm kind of surprised by that." Calder took another swig of his water.

"I'm not. They're a bunch of pussies. They'd never come at you one on one. They know you'd beat their asses and not think twice about doing it." Alex grinned at Calder.

"True," Calder laughed. "Thanks for the heads up."

"It's the least I could do. Trust me when I say that I like you a lot more than the last Alpha."

"Yeah I'm hearing that a lot!"

Two

Daisy rounded the corner deep in thought, not paying attention to anything or anyone around her. The dream she'd had the night before rattled something deep in her core. A blaring horn pulled her from the images replaying in her head, but unfortunately it wasn't in time to save her from plowing into a complete stranger, and knocking them to the ground.

"Oh, my gosh! I'm so sorry. Are you okay? Let me help you up. I wasn't paying attention," Daisy rambled, completely embarrassed by her actions. It was so unlike her to be so careless.

"No worries, dear. I'm sure it was an accident."

The woman stood and brushed herself off. "I'm more worried about you than I am about myself."

"I am so sorry. I should have watched where I was going. The last thing you needed today was to be mowed down on your way to—uh, wherever you're off to this morning."

"Relax, dear." The woman placed a calming hand on Daisy's arm. "I was just going to enjoy a nice hot cup of coffee. Why don't you join me?"

Daisy blinked in surprise. The woman was tiny, standing next to her own five-foot-eight frame. It was a wonder she hadn't killed her when she knocked her down. Yet, there the pixie of a woman stood, all four feet, eleven inches of her. Her blue eyes sparkled with a hint of amusement.

"So what do you say? I promise I won't bite."

"Umm. Sure," she agreed. Why? She had no idea, but some little part of her mind shouted that she needed to go with the woman.

Daisy plastered a smile on her face as she accepted the woman's offer. It wasn't as if she had anything better to do. She was officially on vacation and headed to find coffee anyway.

The woman's bright smile eased any remaining fears Daisy might have had about accepting the invitation. "Good!" She looped her arm around Daisy's and led the way. "There's a little place right around the corner. It's one of my favorites to pop into. I know the owner, and girl, let me tell you—they have the best coffee. And the pastries are to die for."

"Great." Daisy tried to keep the sarcasm out of her voice. "There goes my diet."

The woman gave her a once-over with her stunning blue eyes. "Please. I would die to have your height and curves. You are an absolute beauty, and don't you dare let anyone tell you any differently. I forgot to ask your name, dear?"

Suddenly feeling a bit out of place, Daisy glanced down at the woman holding her arm. "Daisy Parks. And you are?"

"Oh for the love of Christ, my mind must be scattered this morning too. I'm Gerri Wilder. It's nice to meet you, dear."

The tantalizing aroma of fresh coffee washed over Daisy the second she opened the door to the quaint coffee shop. "Ahhh, heaven!"

"Right? I don't know how anyone can function without it. I know I can't." Gerri waved to the woman at the counter before claiming a cozy secluded booth.

Daisy looked around the shop intently, deciding that Gerri was right. The place was absolutely perfect, and nowhere near as crowded as her normal morning pit stop. "You know, I've lived in this area for years and never once knew this place existed."

"Well, now you know. I like this place so much better than some of the big chain shops. The people are so much friendlier, and the crowds are nowhere near as thick. Plus, I think I already mentioned their pasteries and how delicious they are."

"I agree. Even in this city, there's nothing quite like getting your morning brew with a side of attitude."

Gerri laughed. "You're absolutely right. So tell me, dear. Are you off to work this morning, or something else?"

"I'm off for the next two weeks. I finished up a ten-day rotation yesterday. It's been hectic and crazy, so I'm looking forward to the time off."

"What kind of work do you do?" Gerri asked as she motioned for the waitress to take their order.

"I'm an emergency room doctor."

"That sounds like an intense job. What do you like to do in your down time? Is there someone special in your life?"

Daisy paused, unsure of how to answer Gerri. Sure, she seemed sweet and all, but did she want to overload her with the baggage that was Daisy's life? Thankfully she was saved from answering by the waitress's interruption.

"What can I get you?"

***

Gerri was the first to speak again after the waitress left. "I'm sorry. You can tell me to fuck off if you want to. You don't have to answer if it makes you uncomfortable. It's in my nature to be nosey. Especially when it comes to all things love. I really can't seem to help myself."

"It's not that. I just don't want you to think I'm nuts. I've scared many people off by opening my mouth, thinking they actually cared about what I had to say." Daisy eyed up the older woman wondering if she was too good to be true.

"Oh please—I wouldn't have asked if I didn't care. Besides I don't think there's anything you can tell me that I haven't heard before. I may not look like it, but I've been around for a while." Gerri laughed at Daisy's assumption. She felt a strong connection to this girl who had run into her.

Sure, she could have avoided the collision with her. Her wolf had warned her well in advance—

but so had something else. She was destined to meet Daisy. Why? She didn't quite know, but she had a feeling that should would know why soon enough.

"So is there someone special in your life?"

"No. Not recently," Daisy sighed.

Was that a hint of sadness she detected?

"Buck up, dear. There are plenty of handsome men out there who would scoop you off your feet in no time flat! You're stunning with that dark hair and bronzed skin. And those curves—it's enough to make an old woman like me jealous."

"Ha. Hardly. Besides, in case you haven't noticed, I'm not exactly tiny like you. That's what all the rage is today. I'm tall and have curves and love handles, and I swear to Jesus, each of these suckers weighs twenty pounds," Daisy said as she motioned to her chest.

"Please. I know what men are looking for. I run a dating agency and you know what? Not one of my clients has ever complained about a girl with curves. Honey, your body type is exactly what's asked for the most."

Daisy arched an eyebrow. "I find that kind of hard to believe. All the guys I've ever dated have criticized me at some point in our relationship about my curves. Every single one of them. They've all been full of backhanded compliments. You know what I'm talking about, right?"

Her voice dripping with sarcasm, she continued on, "I used to love it when one of my exes said, 'You'd be smoking hot if your ass wasn't so big.' Gerri, I could go on and on with the stories, but it's just not worth it. I'm fine with being single for now. I'm tired of being picked apart by guys who think they're better than everyone else, and don't get me started on their over-opinionated families. I just don't need that sort of drama, so I'm focusing on my career for now and just loving myself and my body."

Gerri thought about what Daisy had said, but—knowing the girl was completely wrong in her outlook on love and relationships—she had to find a way to help her. Daisy may have dated before, but Gerri would bet her ass that she'd never dated the right type of man. Which led to her next question. "Have you ever dated a shifter?"

Daisy looked up at Gerri, puzzled. "A shifter? Umm, no. I'm fully human and pretty certain a requirement of dating someone like that is having the ability to shift into an animal. Which I don't."

Gerri smiled at her naïve comment. "Do you have any shifter friends?"

"No. I haven't lived in this area all that long—well, a few years, but I don't really have any friends. Human or otherwise." Daisy blushed at the admission. "I guess I've gotten used to saying I'm new here or I haven't lived here long. It's kind of been my go-to excuse, even though it's not exactly true anymore."

"Well, now you do." Gerri reached across the table, lacing her fingers with Daisy's. "We were destined to meet today."

***

Daisy had no idea why she was drawn to Gerri, but she was. It was more than her friendly face and her soothing, yet inviting smile. The woman was a firecracker, just like her Aunt Lucy had been before she'd succumbed to cancer.

"Can I ask you something?" Daisy leaned in to whisper the question to Gerri.

"Sure."

"Why did you ask if I've ever dated a shifter? Have you?"

Gerri laughed at her question. "Oh, girl. You are too precious." Gerri fished one of her business cards out of her purse and slid it across the table to Daisy. "I run the Paranormal Dating Agency."

"Wait! What?" Her chin nearly hit the floor. The sassy look on Gerri's face left her speechless.

"My clients are all shifters."

"Wow." Daisy had a million questions and no idea which one to ask first. She'd never met a shifter in person. Well, none that she knew of. It was always possible, but the only way to tell that someone was a shifter was for them to transform from human to animal in front of you—and *that* had certainly never happened. She definitely would have remembered.

"And you were the one worried about scaring *me* away," Gerri joked. "The look on your face right now is priceless."

"Yeah. How about that?" Daisy's mind was blown. "So how does it work? Your dating agency, that is? Are guys in the shifter world like regular human guys?"

"Let's break it down. One question at a time. My service works like any other dating service out there; the only difference is that I specialize in helping shifters find their mates. Men are men, no matter what species, but generally speaking shifters are different with their relationships than humans."

"What do you mean, 'different,' and what's the difference between a mate and a boyfriend or spouse?"

Daisy sat on the edge of her seat waiting for Gerri to answer. She wanted to shout in frustration, anxious to hear the answers. But that would be rude, crass, and uncalled-for, so she sat patiently waiting as Gerri slowly sipped at her coffee before answering.

"Well, for starters, most of my clients have tried the standard dating scene and weren't impressed by it. They are tired of the games and run-around. These people are focused on finding the one person they are destined to spend their lives with—a.k.a. their mate. Think of a mate as your soulmate. The one person that you're supposed to be with, forever."

"That's pretty heavy stuff." Even for Daisy who had always dreamed of finding the one special man who would sweep her off her feet, put a ring on her finger, and spend the rest of his life with her. Things like that just didn't happen for her.

"Indeed it is. But shifters know immediately when they meet their mate. It's kind of like an instant sensation, a recognition that tells them the person they just met is the one they are meant to be with."

"That's kind of odd." Daisy couldn't imagine meeting someone and knowing immediately that they were the person she'd spend the rest of her life with. "What happened to becoming friends, and falling in love?" Not that she'd had much experience with love, but whatever. She was an old-fashioned girl with old-fashioned dating ideas. Like actually leaving the house to go on dates, courting, the guy bringing the girl flowers—the formerly standard, but now very outdated, romantic ideas.

"You'd be surprised how attentive male shifters can be in a relationship."

"Really?" Gerri's simple statement had Daisy fully intrigued.

"Absolutely. The old-school courting usually doesn't happen because a shifter male is very intense when it comes to claiming his mate, but he will always make up for it in other areas. Would you ever consider dating a shifter?"

Daisy thought about the question. Would she? "I'm not sure. Maybe? I'd be so nervous. I'd have no idea how to act around a shifter." Something inside of her tingled at the very thought of the idea of dating a shifter.

"Sure you would. You've been wonderful company the entire time we've been together." Gerri smiled as she revealed the truth.

"You mean you're...?"

"Have been all my life. I tell you what, I have to run. I have a meeting with a client this morning. Why don't you think about it and give me a call? We can set something up if you're interested."

Three

"What do you mean I have thirty days to find a mate? Who came up with this fucking law?" Calder slammed his fist against his desk, outraged by the ridiculous demand that had been forced on him.

Alex ran his fingers through his shaggy blond hair. "Bastards. I knew they were going to try to find some way to keep you from being Alpha."

"Calder, I'm sorry. The Council should have known this was a requirement, but we didn't. The last copy of Twisted Tail laws we had on hand were outdated, and many of them predate Griffin's reign—not that this law isn't archaic. It is, but unfortunately, it exists. And now that it's been brought up as a challenge to the legitimacy of you being Alpha, there's no escaping it. It's pack law. The Alpha must uphold the rules of the pack. Especially the ones that pertain to mating."

Calder saw the sadness in his dear friend's eyes. Gus Eklund—or 'old man,' as he often teasingly called him—was more than just a friend, more than a mentor. The older man had watched over him for years, acting as an informal uncle with whom he'd enjoyed a close relationship. It was Gus who had lead the charge for Calder to take the reins at Twisted Tail after the death of their former Alpha Griffin Engle.

"I know Gus. I just don't know how it's possible. Thirty days isn't a lot of time to find your true mate."

"No, it's not. But I don't think it's impossible. I think it can be done. You're just going to need a little bit of help."

Calder laughed at the thought of someone helping him to find his mate. "I think you've finally lost it, old man. I'm not so sure that's how it works in this day and age. I don't think I can send a proxy to find or claim my mate, and Odin knows I can't leave pack territory right now. Not with all the work that needs to be done around here. Besides, I haven't named a second-in-command yet. I'm quite literally stuck here until I set up a proper chain of command."

Gus pulled a large manila envelope from his briefcase and handed it to Calder. "I want you to know the Council is dedicated to helping you succeed, and to helping everyone here at Twisted Tail. We've set up a trust that you may use as you see fit to rebuild the pack. This should help when it comes to hiring people to make the needed repairs across the territory, and any other maintenance work that needs to be done. I'm sure it will help motivate those within the pack to get back to work as well, if they are able-bodied. Our hope was to provide the necessary means to get the work done; that way we could free up your time, so you can focus on rebuilding and strengthening the pack itself, not just the buildings and structures."

Calder sucked in a deep breath and opened the envelope, unsure of the extent of what Gus's statement meant. A volley of emotions bounded through him. *"Thank you, Odin,"* Calder said to his wolf.

The old man had come through for him, big time, in ways he'd never envisioned. Money was nothing to the Council. Having been around for thousands of years with the ability to operate in complete secrecy, they had more than they'd ever need, more than they could ever hope to spend. But to a struggling pack like Twisted Tail it meant their continued survival. Not only had the Council made sure they would survive—if Calder played his cards right, they would now have an opportunity to thrive.

"I don't know what to say. This is—" Calder's words tumbled out of his mouth.

"It's nothing. Get your pack together and on its feet again. It's the least we can do for the people here, after failing them by believing everything Griffin had told us and not following through when we had doubts or questions. The hardships this pack has had to endure are over. I know if anyone can lead this pack into a new era, it's you."

"Thank you, but I'm afraid none of it will do much good if I don't find my mate before I run out of time."

"That's what they're counting on." Alex, who had been silent during the exchange between Gus and Calder, finally spoke up.

"What do you know about this?" Gus asked.

"Not enough. They tend to zip their lips around me these days. But from what I've been able to figure out, Jason and a few others—who lived pretty comfortably under Griffin—are pissed the money and drugs are gone, and so is their way of life. They thrived under Griffin because they were a bunch of thugs. Now that they have to get out there and work—well, they're not too happy about it. What they're too stupid to see is how much better off we've been since Griffin's death. People are no longer afraid to let their kids outside to play. Women can walk around town without being bombarded with crude comments or fearing for their safety. The difference is night and day."

"The transformation in the last few weeks has been pretty amazing," Calder said. "It's nice to see people learning to trust each other again and kicking the fears they carried for so long to the curb. We can't slow the progress that's been made, and if I leave for any amount of time to run off and search for a mate, I expect it'll be like taking ten steps backward. Not exactly what we want to happen."

Calder had to trust his gut on this. He couldn't leave Twisted Tail. Too many people were depending on him to keep the peace. He'd made a promise to them. One that he was bound to keep.

Gus nodded in agreement. "Right. So you have to find your mate in thirty days, and you can't leave pack territory."

"Exactly." Calder rubbed his forehead, a stress-induced habit he had picked up long ago.

"So we do the only thing we can do." Gus pulled a business card from his wallet and handed it to Calder.

"Paranormal Dating Agency? What's this?"

"If anyone can find your mate by the deadline, it's Gerri Wilder. She's the best of the best, and you need to give her a call."

"You can't be serious." Calder laughed at his friend's suggestion. He'd accused Gus of losing his mind before, now it looked as if the old man had indeed lost his damn mind.

"As a heart attack, kid."

"A dating agency? How the hell is that supposed to help? It's not like I can run out and meet up with however many women they have on their list."

"She's the only one who can help you right now." Gus reiterated his point.

"Great. I'm going to end up with a weird mail-order bride or a psycho or something." Calder picked up the phone and shooed everyone out of the room. "This is embarrassing enough. I don't need an audience."

Four

I wonder what it would be like to date a shifter? Daisy thought about the conversation she'd had with Gerri the previous morning. Could she actually go through with it? Pacing around her living room contemplating the question was pointless and she knew it, but the truth was Gerri had sparked Daisy's interest in dating—an interest she hadn't felt in forever.

That was a good thing? Right?

Gerri had reminded her that she was alone. She woke up alone. Ate breakfast, lunch, and dinner alone. Went to the movies alone. After her last relationship, Daisy had decided to take a break from dating. She had needed time to find her footing in the world again, and she did just that. Grabbing the bull by the horns, she packed up her shit and moved, taking the first job she was offered, far away from the tiny town in Wisconsin she had grown up in.

The relationship ended the day her boyfriend had said, "As soon as you lose some weight, I'll take you home to meet my parents." Yeah, that was enough for her to end it right there, on the spot. Afterwards she'd cried for weeks, vowing never to put herself in that position again.

And she hadn't.

She'd sworn off dating until she shed some pounds. And she had. She had gotten into the habit of walking daily, and eating healthier, but she was still curvy. Her confidence had risen, but was it enough to put herself out there again? Even if Gerri swore to her that shifters loved curvy women?

A few of the guys she worked with at the hospital had asked her out on dates. She smiled politely and turned each of them down, too afraid to feel the sting of rejection once again. But maybe this time would be different. Maybe Gerri was right. Maybe she needed to date a different kind of guy.

Before Daisy lost her nerve, she grabbed Gerri's business card and her phone from her purse. *Here goes nothing.*

"Daisy, I'm so glad to hear from you."

Daisy's heart pounded. Butterflies—and not the good ones—danced in her belly. "Hi, Gerri. I—uhh... umm." Daisy cleared her throat.

"Are you okay, dear?"

She sucked in a deep breath, hoping like hell it would calm her nerves. It didn't. "Yes, just nervous." Opting for honesty, she forged ahead. "I want to know more about your dating service."

"Wonderful! I have just the person I'd like you to meet. You said you were on vacation from work, right?"

"Yes, but what does that have to do with anything?" Daisy asked, confused by Gerri's line of questioning. What did being on vacation have to do with meeting someone? All she had asked for in the first place was more information. Talk about speedy service!

"The man who I think would be perfect for you is in a bit of a quandary. He's the new Alpha of Twisted Tail pack, and he's looking for someone to meet him there. You would spend a few days together, getting to know one another."

"Umm, that's a bit more than I had bargained for right off the bat. I was expecting maybe dinner or something easy like that. You know, a standard date."

Gerri laughed. "Nothing is standard when it comes to dating a shifter, dear. Think of it this way. Lodging will be provided. You'll have a chance to get out of town for a few days to clear your head. When's the last time you got out of the city for a long weekend? And if you guys hit it off, great. If not, no big deal. You had some time away from everyone and everything in the fresh country air. If nothing else, you'll be recharged and ready to go back to work when you get back."

Daisy's pacing resumed. Panic crept through her veins. A date was one thing. Going to spend several days with a complete stranger was something altogether different that she found scary as hell. "Is that safe to do? I don't want to end up trapped in someone's well in their basement or something."

Gerri laughed at her response. "Sure it is, dear. All of my clients are thoroughly vetted. I run full background checks and contact each reference they provide, personally. Not only that, but shifters, especially wolves, are extremely protective of their women—annoyingly so, at times. Once you cross over into pack land, you'll be safer than you would be anywhere else in the world."

Without letting another thought pass through her mind, Daisy agreed. "I'll do it."

"Great! Do you have a pen? I'll give you the address and directions."

Daisy's heart sped up as she grabbed a pen and paper. "Ready."

OMG! I can't believe I'm going to go through with this!

After the call, Daisy felt a sense of excitement—and a bit of fear—as she rushed around the house to pack a suitcase for her trip. She'd never done anything so crazy in all her well-thought-out, well-planned life.

Doubt began to creep into her mind with each outfit she selected and packed. What if she didn't get along with Calder? What if he didn't like her? What if he was as ugly as homemade sin?

She pushed back against the thoughts, refusing to give into her fears. She had committed to going. Come hell or high water, she was bound and determined to hold up her end of the bargain. Closing the lid on her suitcase, Daisy swallowed the nervousness dancing in her belly and headed for her car, knowing it was now or never.

The road trip to Twisted Tail gave her a lot of time to think about *exactly* what she was doing.

Too much time. All the bad decisions Daisy had made in her previous relationships ran through her mind, reminding her exactly why she'd taken a hiatus from dating. She had been tempted to turn the car around several times, but she gritted her teeth and continued on. It was almost as if some unseen force urged her to continue on her journey toward the unknown.

Five

The lack of sleep over the past few weeks had finally caught up with Calder. He was dead on his feet, and thankfully headed home for the night. The assistance from Gus, his workload had been eased drastically. Having enough money to hire contractors to do the maintenance and repair work around Twisted Tail was a godsend. The old man had really come through for him, and just when he had needed help the most.

In all honesty, he would have thought that he'd have a little bit of breathing room now that there was less construction work he had to do personally. Wrong. Calder was more stressed than ever thanks to the rising pack tensions—and then there was the whole 'finding a mate' issue.

He wasn't sure what to make of his conversation with Gerri. On one hand it had sounded promising, she'd told him that finding his mate and sending her to Twisted Tail would be a piece of cake, but he wasn't holding his breath waiting for a damn miracle that, in his mind, was unlikely to occur. Keeping the sarcasm out of his voice after her statement had taken effort, but somehow he'd managed. After all, Gus had assured him that Gerri Wilder was the best in the business and swore she could find a mate for Satan himself, should he ever be on the market.

Calder pulled up to the wrought iron gate in front of the Alpha's well-kept home. There was no doubt the log home was stunning, with its high peaked roof and wrap-around porch. Griffin had spared no expense when it came to the home's construction, surrounding himself with every possible luxury. It was totally out of place compared to the rest of the modest homes situated on pack lands.

Living there for the past few weeks had left Calder feeling out of sorts, knowing his pack lived in such dilapidated houses. That's why his first priority had been working feverishly on the desperately needed repairs and long-overdue updates around the territory.

Calder got out of his truck and opened the gate. Out of habit he sniffed the air, searching for any threats. *"We really need to get our second in place so we can start appointing enforcers,"* Calder said to his wolf.

"I would trust Alex with our lives. As for the rest of them, the jury's still out."

"Agreed."

Calder pulled his truck through the gate and exited the vehicle once more, this time to close the gate back up. He was tired of looking over his shoulder every second of every day, waiting for the inevitable attack to come, thanks to the few bad seeds left over from the previous Alpha. He knew exactly who they were, and while Alex didn't think they would challenge his position, Calder knew they would. It was only a matter of time. One way or another, they'd come. *"And I'd damn well better be ready when they do,"* he thought.

Scenting no immediate danger, Calder climbed back in his truck and headed down the long wooded driveway. His stomach grumbled, reminding him the sandwich he'd had for lunch hadn't quite cut it, and it was long past dinner time. But first things first. A nice hot shower.

"Someone's here." His wolf sounded the alarm in his mind.

Rolling down the window he drew in a deep breath, trying to identify the threat his wolf had detected. The smell of fresh-cut wildflowers filled Calder's nose. His wolf whined at the scent as it filtered down to him.

Wary of who might be waiting for him, Calder slowly rounded the last curve in the driveway to see a bright yellow Camaro with black racing stripes parked in front of his house. Coming to a quick stop, he hopped out of his truck, ready to confront the person who had trespassed on his land—but the car was empty. Calder glanced around the property before noticing several lights on in the house—lights he was certain he had turned off.

His wolf spurred him on, pushing him to sprint up the steps then through the front door. The animal didn't seem upset by the intruder. Not in the least. It was much more of an immense curiosity that filled the animal. Calder tried to figure out what his wolf was up to, but he had no idea why that particular scent had his beast so intrigued.

The smell of fresh roasted meat set off a new round of grumbling from his stomach. The man may have been distracted by the thought of a home-cooked meal, but not the wolf. He had smelled something much more inviting. As much as Calder wanted to investigate the tantalizing aroma coming from the kitchen, his legs seemed to move of their own volition, demanding he locate the source of the fresh wildflowers that had his wolf all worked up.

As he made his way deeper into the house searching for the intruder, a singsong voice floated in the air.

"A woman." Astonishment crashed over Calder. His strong legs suddenly lost all coordination and were replaced by what felt like those of a newborn deer. Another step on shaky legs sent him crashing into the wall as he worked his way closer to the tantalizing sound.

"Is someone there?" the female voice called out.

Calder opened his mouth to speak, but his tongue was too heavy and thick; no words were forthcoming. He forged on, using the wall as a support, desperately needing to confirm that his dreamlike state was a reality and not some twisted trick of majik played on him by someone wanting to see him fail.

The singing resumed as Calder slowly worked his way to the master bedroom— hoping and expecting to see a divine goddess stretched across his bed, lying in wait for his homecoming. Instead he found the door to the master bath ajar.

He knew he should give her some privacy, but honor be damned, he had to see the woman who possessed the harmonious voice that was keeping him in a state of awe. Leaning against the doorframe, Calder felt his heart skip a beat, maybe two—and his wolf screamed in his head, *"MINE!"*

The amount of sheer willpower it took not to launch himself directly on the dark-haired, bronze-skinned beauty in the bathtub was monumental. Like serious effort, gold-medal-award shit.

Calder sucked in a deep breath, mesmerized by the droplets of water that trickled down her chest and over her full breasts as she slowly sat forward. Feeling like a voyeur, he tried to avert his eyes but failed as billows of steam rose from her heated skin. He tucked his fingers deep into his tight pockets to keep from reaching out and seeing if her skin was indeed as soft as it looked. His cock grew painfully hard as he imagine climbing into the tub behind her and pushing her hair to the side, trailing soft kisses over her neck and shoulders.

A war with his animal raged within. The wolf wanted to mark and claim her as his own, taking what the Fates decreed as his. The man was much more cautious, not wanting to terrify her, sensing she held no majik of her own. She was as human as could be—a thought that should have sent him running for the hills, but didn't. He had full trust in the Fates that this woman, in all her human glory, was made for him, and him alone.

Six

All of Daisy's tension from the long drive evaporated the second she dipped her toe into the oversized bathtub. When she'd first arrived at the address Gerri had given her, a fresh wave of panic almost sent her speeding back to her tiny apartment in the city. But she held her ground, thinking instead that if some lonely wolf wanted to treat her to the lap of luxury for a few days, she was game. After all, what did she have to lose? It wasn't like she expected to fall madly in love at first sight or some crazy shit like that. She read romance novels for fun here and there, but knew they were nothing more than random fantasies dreamt up by people far more creative than her—and besides, her life didn't even come close to the sexy women always cast as the heroines in the garden-variety romance books she found tucked neatly behind action/adventure books at her local grocery store.

She found the front door unlocked, just as Gerri had promised, and made her way inside. Her jaw nearly hit the damn floor on her solo tour of the gorgeous log home. Private accommodations were one thing, but this place was off the charts, with windows stretching from the floor to the three-story ceiling, beautiful hardwood floors extending from one end of the home to the other, and a large library packed with leather-bound volumes that left her well and truly speechless. She could spend her entire vacation poring over the vast texts housed on perfectly framed bookcases.

And then she spied the master bedroom with its glorious four-poster bed and puffy comforter. Daisy couldn't help but launch herself halfway across the room onto the bed just to see if it was as comfy as it looked. Heaven help her, it was.

Just when she thought life couldn't get any better, she stumbled into the bathroom to find a glorious jetted bathtub that beckoned her as if she were a mermaid who'd been stuck on dry land for far too long.

Her stomach grumbled, letting her know that food would be required in the very near future, and she had to agree. Promising the tub she'd be back shortly, she went off in search of the kitchen. The sparsely filled fridge would need to be remedied if she planned on staying there for any length of time. Searching through the pantry and freezer, she found enough ingredients to throw together a quick—but guaranteed to be yummy—beef stew. Filling the crock pot with all the fixings and setting it on 'high,' she headed back to the bath in a state of sheer excitement.

Stripping off her jeans and T-shirt, Daisy adjusted the temperature of the water and climbed in, reveling in the heat of the water as it quickly surrounded her. She had no idea how much time had passed as she soaked, enjoying the gentle massage of the jets pulsing over her skin, nor did she care. She closed her eyes and began softly singing the catchy tune that had been stuck in her brain for days.

Suddenly she shot forward, thinking she'd heard the sound of a door closing. She called out, but no one answered. "Huh. Must be my imagination," she said out loud. Daisy managed to shake off the notion that someone had entered the home, leaning back once again and letting the sweet melody flow from her lips until she felt as if she were being watched.

Cocking her head to the side and slowly peeling her eyes open, she sucked in a deep breath when she saw a stranger standing in the doorway watching her every move. Daisy gasped at the sight of the man before her, and not just because he was leaning against the door frame staring at her with his mouth agape. Oh no. It was much more than that. Every hormone in her body sprang to life with one glance in his direction.

Her eyes roamed greedily over the man, sizing him up. Starting at the top and working her way down, Daisy catalogued each of his remarkable features, committing them to memory, from his dark shaggy hair—which she itched to run her fingers through—to his high cheekbones, strong jaw, and Grecian nose. His shoulders nearly too wide to fit through the door frame, he leaned against it at an angle. A black T-shirt stretched over his broad shoulders and thick chest to meet his perfectly defined arms, which she wanted nothing more than to feel wrapped tight around her.

She drew a shaky breath as her eyes dared even lower to his trim waist, and the firm backside encased in a pair of faded blue jeans that was barely visible. Daisy bit her lip and tried to glance away as she spied the bulge that became more evident as he shifted his stance.

Sweet Jesus, the man exuded an air of sexuality like she'd never felt radiating from another male. He looked raw and dangerous—and built for sin. She had no problems imagining all of that raw sexuality stretched over her body. His rippling muscles flexing to—

"Stop that, you little perv! You don't even know the man and here you are fantasizing about him." She thought as she looked away sharply, embarrassed by her brazen behavior. She opened her mouth to speak, then quickly snapped it shut again. What could she possibly say to make the situation any less awkward than it already was?

"Nothing! Zip. Zero. Zilch."

With that thought in mind, Daisy did the only thing she could think of. She folded her legs and allowed her body to slip slowly under the water, hoping like hell that when she came back up for air, the sexy stranger would be nowhere in sight.

"Do you make a habit of breaking into homes and trying to drown yourself in the owner's bathtub?" The stranger's amber eyes sparkled as he pulled her, flailing and sputtering, from the water that she'd hoped to seek refuge under.

Daisy swatted him away. His hands were far too warm on her skin, and she had to break contact before she warped into a babbling lunatic. She needed her wits about her.

More now than ever.

"Your home?" Daisy asked, confused by his statement, knowing damn well she had triple-checked the address Gerri had given her. She had even called to confirm it when she arrived. "There must be some mistake! I was given this address by a friend who—" Her voice trailed off. What the hell was she supposed to say? And how desperate did she want to look in front of the male she'd just undressed with her eyes?

The stranger cocked his head, waiting for her to continue. "Go on."

"Well—I was given this address to stay at for a few days while I met someone." Daisy grabbed a fluffy white towel and quickly covered her chest, suddenly embarrassed by his nearness and her complete state of undress.

"Why don't you get dressed and meet me in the kitchen? We can discuss this matter further there."

Daisy bobbed her head in agreement, feeling like a complete idiot.

Seven

Feeling like he had less control than he'd had in the throes of puberty, Calder hurried to the kitchen and away from the woman in his bathtub. He needed a moment to rein in his wolf before the animal acted on his pure, raw, and base instinct of claiming their mate. If the woman were another shifter, he would have surrendered control to the wolf in a heartbeat, but she wasn't. She was human.

The very thought made his head spin. His whole life, he'd been led to believe his mate would be some sort of shifter, like himself, or at least in possession of some majikal abilities of her own.

But no—oh no, there would be no such luck for him. The Fates appeared to have had other plans for him.

Even as he stood in the kitchen, leaning against the counter, his cock was as hard as a motherfucking rock. The second he'd caught sight of her, he knew there was no turning back, human or not. Plain and simple, she was his mate and he would claim her. She may not have any idea how the whole mating process worked, but she was about to get a crash course on the subject to get her up to speed. Something that needed to happen really fucking quick.

"So, uhh—this is pretty awkward."

Calder had scented her approach long before she'd entered the room. "Indeed. Why don't you start by telling me who you are and what brought you to my home?" Crossing his arms over his chest, he gave her his best stern look, needing to discern the truth from her. He replayed his last call with Gerri in his mind. The woman she was supposed to send, Daisy, wasn't supposed to show up for another day. Could this be her?

His eyes roamed over every inch of her luscious curvy body. Her long dark hair fell to the middle of her back, and his mouth went dry as he pictured it cascading over them as she straddled him, leaned in to him, taking every inch of his cock deep inside of her. Her full breasts and luscious hips did nothing to ease the strain of his cock against his tight jeans, imagining her thick thighs wrapped tight around his body. And those bright pink toes, just like little jellybeans—oh, how he longed to suck each one of them into his mouth.

His wolf snorted. *"Daisy, huh? She smells like her name."*

Calder silently agreed with his wolf. After all, it was pretty damn ironic.

Full of spunk and sass, the woman dared to mock his stance, looking as if she were ready to play hardball with a shifter who was easily a foot taller than her, and close to double her weight.

She even had the nerve to lift her little chin in the air when she opened her mouth to speak. "My name is Daisy Parks. Gerri Wilder sent me to meet Calder Lorenson," she said with an exasperated huff.

"Ahhh, so you're the infamous Daisy Parks that Gerri's been gushing about." He smiled—she was indeed the one who'd been sent by Gerri. That knowledge alone helped to calm any lingering fears floating around in his mind.

Her full lush lips gaped open at his statement. "Are you Calder?"

"I am." This time he flashed his best brilliant white smile, hoping to convey an air of charm instead of the tougher stance he had taken when she'd first walked into the kitchen.

***

Daisy grabbed on to the side of the table, suddenly needing support, her legs quaking underneath of her. *Holy hell!* she thought, knowing she was in way over her head with the hunky homeowner who was searching for his mate. Gerri had told her a few things about male shifters, but not much. First and foremost, it would have been awesome had Gerri forewarned her that Calder wasn't just hot, he was smoking-fucking-hot, like straight up sizzling, and there she was in a pair of well-worn yoga pants and an old tank top, looking like a drowned river-rat with her long hair dripping down her back.

Every ounce of her flesh zinged to life just being in the same room with him, not to mention the fact that, when he'd yanked her out of the tub, she'd felt a jolt of awareness the second his fingers had wrapped around her wrist.

"Are you okay?"

Suddenly looking concerned for her well-being, Calder approached her slowly, his hands up in surrender.

Shaking her head to clear her thoughts, Daisy desperately worked to regain some sort of composure. *Way to go moron,* her conscience shouted. She cleared her throat. "Yeah." *Great,* she thought, horrified by the squeak in her voice. "Just surprised to find you here. Gerri told me I would have my own private accommodations. I assumed she meant I'd have the house to myself. I am so sorry for intruding."

Daisy felt like a complete and utter ass, absolutely stupid. How could she have strolled into a stranger's house and made herself at home, cooking dinner, lounging in his bathtub for hours? *Fuck!* She covered her face with her hands, hot tears threatening to embarrass her further.

She nearly jumped out of her skin when she felt the heat from his hand press lightly against her shoulder.

"Hey. It's okay. No harm, no foul. It wasn't so bad coming home to a home-cooked meal and a sexy woman in my bathtub."

Sexy? Ha! she thought. "I am so sorry. I feel like an idiot. I don't know what is wrong with me. I shouldn't have assumed. I won't be upset if you want me to leave."

Eight

Leave? She was nuts for even thinking that? The mere thought of her getting up and walking out of the door was simply unacceptable. Now that she was in his home, there was no way he was letting her go that quickly, especially not because of a stupid mix-up. No way in hell. "No! I don't want you to leave."

Calder quickly adjusted his tone. "Sorry, it's just that I was expecting you tomorrow, not today. So when I came in and found someone here, I was on high alert. I guess all the adrenaline is still rushing through me." The lie burned his tongue as he spoke it, but he wasn't about to tell her the truth, fearing he'd come off too intense and scare her away. "Gerri told me you'd be here on Thursday."

He watched as Daisy cocked her head to the side and quickly opened her mouth then closed it, deciding on if she should speak or not. "Umm—it *is* Thursday. I think your days might be a bit off."

Calder stomped over to the fridge to look at the calendar, the sole item hanging there by one lone magnet. Stunned by the fact that he'd somehow walked around all day thinking it was Wednesday, it was his turn to feel like an idiot. "Huh. How about that, it is. Well, now *I* feel like an ass." He turned back to Daisy, who busted into a full-on belly laugh.

"We make quite the pair already, don't we?" she managed to chuckle between laughing fits.

"We sure do." Finding her laugh contagious, Calder gave in and laughed with her, something he hadn't done since he'd moved to Twisted Tail. Maybe the old saying—'laughter is the best medicine'—was right, because in that one tiny moment with a girl he barely knew, he'd felt the weight of the stress he'd been buried under since taking over as Alpha rise and lift slowly away from his shoulders.

When the laughing finally faded away, Calder was the first to speak. "I'd planned on taking you out for dinner tonight, but"—he motioned to the crock pot—"that smells amazing, and I can't even begin to remember the last time I ate something homemade."

"Really? You don't like to cook?" She looked shocked at his admission.

"I wish I knew how to cook, God knows I do, but somehow I end up burning everything I try to make. Even a simple pan of boiling water ends up as a smoking pot."

"I don't mind cooking while I'm here. Granted, we'll need to hit up a grocery store, but it'll be fun. I find the whole process of making new creations very relaxing, probably because of the repetitive motions."

His mind went straight to the gutter, as did his wolf's. *"I'll give her some repetitive motions."*

"There I go assuming again. I should have said, if it's okay with you."

He gave a nod and an agreeable grin. "Only if you're comfortable doing so, and not every meal. I'd like to take you out as well. We don't have a huge selection of restaurants here in town, but the few we have are good."

"I'd like that. I can't wait to see more of the area. I kind of had tunnel vision on the drive in, just wanting to make sure I found the right place."

He wanted to lay it all out for Daisy, to let her know exactly what she'd be getting into by becoming his mate.

"I have to warn you, the pack is undergoing a lot of changes right now. I'm the new Alpha and I haven't been here long, so please excuse the mess with all the construction going on. The last Alpha left the pack in pretty rough shape, but I have high hopes that I can pull it all together and get everyone back on their feet."

"I grew up in an itty-bitty town in rural Wisconsin, so small-town life isn't a problem for me. It's quaint and quiet, a lifestyle that I find myself missing more and more. I thought city life would be neat, that a country girl like me could handle it, but yeah—it's pretty hard to get used to, and talk about serious culture shock. I miss walking outside and seeing grass, and trees instead of concrete and traffic. And stars. Oh, how I've missed actually being able to see the stars in the sky! I've been in the city now for a few years and I still feel like I'm stumbling my way through everything. My life has been a series of trials and errors when it comes to big city living. Sorry, I'm babbling—I tend to do that when I'm nervous."

"I like hearing about your life. Since I moved here I've been pretty isolated, and I definitely haven't had anyone to just sit and shoot the shit with. But I have to ask, why are you nervous?"

Calder sucked in a deep breath, scenting the air around him. His wolf didn't pick up even the slightest hint of fear—curiosity, yes; fear, no. He pulled up a seat next to her at the table, realizing that, imposing as he was, his size may have been part of the problem.

He bit back a groan as she twirled a long lock of hair around in her fingertips, looking as if she were trying to work out a complicated problem.

"It's embarrassing really. I'm sure you knew the second you met me that I'm not like you. Er—what I mean is that I'm not a shifter, I'm human. Anyway, until I met Gerri, I'd never been around someone like her… or you."

Calder loved the blush that covered her cheeks as she tried to spit out her brave admission that she'd never been around shifters. "I'm an open book; ask me any questions you'd like. I promise not to be offended."

Nine

Daisy quickly perked up, her curiosity spiking to an all-time high. She had a million and one questions, but didn't want to come off sounding stupid, nor was it her intent to offend him or Gerri with her silly curiosities. "Are you sure?"

Threads of uncertainty tugged at her mind, because she had no idea what was considered proper etiquette with shifters, but how was a girl to know if she didn't ask?

Calder managed to quash her fears with a soft smile. "Absolutely. Why don't we do this, so we can get to know one another? You ask me a question, then I'll ask you a question in return. We'll work on a *quid pro quo* kind of system."

Daisy mulled over his offer. It seemed fair enough. Besides, it wasn't like she had anything to hide; her life up to this point had been boring as hell. "Okay, that sounds fair. Why don't we grab a bowl of stew first and ask questions over dinner?"

"Perfect!" Daisy bit her bottom lip, watching as Calder stood and stretched before crossing the room to the cabinets. Her eyes roamed greedily once again over the expanse of his backside. Her breath caught in her throat when he reached up to grab a couple of bowls from the shelf, his tight black T-shirt killing her with each stretch across the muscles that flexed and rippled with every move he made.

"You're going to have some too, right?"

"Yep, sorry. I'm coming." *Ha! I wish!* she thought. She had never been so turned on just by sitting next to a man, but there was something about the sexy shifter that called to her like no other ever had. One glance in his direction, one sexy smile was all it took for her hormones to kick in and demand they be given full attention.

She snapped out of her lust-induced haze long enough to give the stew one last stir, then fill their bowls to the top while Calder filled two glasses with ice and water from the fridge.

A few minutes later, and after they both settled at the table, Daisy wondered anew where she should start.

"This is really good, by the way," Calder said after his first bite of the meaty stew. "Ask away." He motioned for Daisy to start off the first round of questions.

Blurting out the first question that popped into her mind, she started with. "Can you really turn into an animal?"

Daisy gasped as Calder pushed his chair away from the table and stood. Shocked at her own impudence, she quickly apologized. "I'm sorry, of course you can. It's just that with me being fully human, I've never seen a shifter—well, shift. All of this is so new to me and so fascinating, my human mind is having a hard time processing all the majik that must surround your life."

The atmosphere in the room changed, and before she could say another word, a cool breeze whipped through the kitchen. The spot where Calder stood shimmered with majik that made the hair on her arms stand on end. One second the sexy man stood in front of her, and the next an enormous grey wolf stood, eyeing her up.

Her mouth flew open to say something, anything, as the wolf slowly stalked toward her. Her mind worked overtime absorbing the change that had just taken place right before her eyes. She snapped her mouth shut, determined not to scream in fear. God knows she wanted to leap up off of the damn chair and run as fast as she could and as far as her legs would carry her, but she kept her ass firmly planted, knowing he had simply answered the question she'd asked.

Her Gram's voice popped into her head. "Don't ask questions you don't want the answers to, honey bun."

Daisy had never understood that particular saying and what her Gram had meant until now. If she was going to ask questions, she had to be tough enough to accept the truthful answer.

The wolf whined, pulling Daisy from her train of thoughts. Shock twisted through her when he laid his head on her leg, his nose precariously close to her crotch.

"Watch it, buddy. Wolf or not, I'll not think twice about smacking you in the nose if you deserve it."

The wolf huffed, his ears twitching.

"How had I not noticed your eyes before now?" Tiny gold flecks highlighted deep amber eyes, which she imagined held a vast amount of knowledge in all things ancient and majikal. Without even thinking about it, she reached out to touch his fur, needing to see if it was as soft and as thick as it looked.

The wolf whined again, seeming to like her touch.

"You like your ears scratched, don't you." Daisy laughed.

The wolf stepped back as she laughed.

Fear raced through her and, thinking she'd offended the animal, she rushed to once again apologize. "I didn't mean to insinuate that it was a bad thing. I thought it was cute."

Daisy blinked as the odd majikal shimmer she'd seen moments ago reappeared and surrounded the animal. She nearly jumped out of her skin when she heard Calder's voice.

"Actually it does feel good. If you had kept it up, I would have been snoring in seconds flat."

Daisy giggled, once again surprised by his answer.

"Now you owe me two answers." Calder took his seat and another bite of his stew.

"That was incredible. Thank you for giving me that first experience."

"You're welcome. So how did you meet Gerri?"

"I literally ran into her."

"What do you mean?" Calder looked at her quizzically, perhaps surprised by her answer.

"I was headed out for coffee one morning and rounded the corner, not paying attention to where I was going. Next thing I knew I plowed right into the poor woman."

"Huh. That's pretty odd."

"Why is that?" Daisy tilted her head to the side, wondering what would be so odd about running into someone on a crowded sidewalk.

Calder challenged her. "Another question—you'll owe me another answer."

"Fine." Damn it, she wanted to know what he'd meant by that statement.

"Wolves—well, all shifters really—have heightened senses. We know there is someone near well before we see them. For instance, I knew someone was on the property the second I got out of my truck to close the gate."

His answer startled her, and her face must have shown it.

"We have heightened senses of hearing and smell. Trust me when I tell you Gerri would have sensed you or smelled you long before you got anywhere near her. So, yeah. I think it's odd that she *let* you run into her."

"I'm going to owe you a million answers, but I have to know—why would she let me bump into her, then?"

Calder shrugged, "I'm not certain. I've never met her in person, but if I had to guess, I'd say it was because she scented you and knew there was something different about you, something her majik told her not to ignore."

"Interesting."

"My turn." Calder flashed her a sexy smile before asking his next question. "Why did you agree to come here? Especially if you had never been around shifters before?"

Well, that was a loaded question if she'd ever heard one. Daisy debated internally for a minute, struggling with how honest she should be before she finally spoke, "I guess you can blame it all on curiosity." Going for flat-out honesty she braced herself, letting the words flow from her lips. "I've never had much luck in the dating arena, at all. The guys I've dated haven't always been nice, but what I never understood was, if they weren't happy with my size why did they even bother to date me to begin with? Why did they all try to change who I was? Why could they never be happy with me?"

And there it was: all the questions she'd walked away from every relationship with, laid out for a complete stranger to ponder.

All the improvements to her self-esteem that she'd worked so hard to make over the years were suddenly stripped away, leaving her feeling once more like the only fat girl in a sea of skinny models.

Daisy pushed the stew around in her bowl. She had no desire left to eat her dinner, though she'd barely eaten all day.

Ten

Anger pulsed through Calder. Not because of Daisy's admission—because she'd been treated like shit in the past, by complete assholes who he'd like to find and slaughter for hurting his mate. How a guy, any guy, could look at her and think she was anything but absolutely stunning was beyond him.

She had to know there was nothing wrong with her, right? But one look at the depth of the sadness in her eyes spoke volumes. His beautiful Daisy had believed every fucking hurtful word those morons had ever said. That just wouldn't do.

"I strongly believe that we go through life meeting a series of people who are horribly wrong for us, because we're caught up in the age-old struggle of wanting to find our soulmate. So we spend our lives with someone, forcing a warped and twisted relationship on ourselves for the sake of not being alone and we're surprised when it blows up."

Calder combed his fingers through his hair, praying what he'd said made sense to Daisy. He needed her to know the guys in her past would never have been right for her, not because there was anything wrong with her, but because she was his mate, destined for him and him alone. "When that one special person comes along—the one you're meant to be with—he'll never make you feel the way those losers did."

"I suppose you're right. It just hasn't made my life any easier."

He didn't like the fact that he'd made her sad.

His wolf whined in his head. *"Cheer her up, asshole."*

"Enough with the heavy talk, let's lighten the mood back up. I believe you had a few more questions for me?" Maybe if he could get her talking, he could get her smiling again—at least, that was his short-term goal when it came to his beautiful mate.

Calder held his breath, waiting to see if Daisy would shake off the shame she felt and open up to him again. Just when he was ready to give up and call it a night, she spoke.

"Does the transformation hurt? You know, when you shift?"

"Not usually. When I choose to shift there is no pain involved, but if I'm forced to shift because of an injury it can be excruciating."

"What types of injuries would cause you to shift like you described?" The doctor in her couldn't help herself, she just had to ask.

"Any severe or life threatening injury, really. Granted we heal faster than humans but we still have our vulnerabilities. Daisy seemed to mull over his answer before asking her next question. "Are you afraid of getting stuck in wolf form?"

That question made him smile—not because it was a silly question, but because she glanced away shyly as the words left her mouth, almost as if getting trapped in an animal form would be her greatest fear. "Not at all. My wolf and I work together to accomplish any task thrown at us. He would never try to take on the human tasks, and I would never try to take over his. Does that make sense?"

"Sort of."

Daisy brushed a stray strand of hair away from her face, not knowing how such a simple act left Calder wanting to pull her into his arms and never let go. It took every ounce of strength he possessed not to scoop her up, toss her in his bed and pound his cock so deep into her that she forgot all about the guys who'd wronged her in the past.

"Wait, can you and your wolf... er... talk to each other?"

"Yes, all the time."

"Huh. That's pretty interesting. What does your wolf think about me?"

"Will you let me show you?" Calder pushed his chair away from the table and stood, holding his hand out to Daisy. He could've easily told her that his wolf wanted nothing more than to kiss and touch every inch of her body, but he didn't want to say it with words that might fall on deaf ears. He wanted to show her that his wolf had only one thing on his mind since the very second he'd picked up her scent.

***

Daisy looked at Calder's outstretched hand, not knowing exactly what he was asking, or what he wanted to show her. But he had managed to once again spark her curiosity. The man fascinated her on every level. She'd dated plenty of guys in the past and not one of them had ever managed to break through the walls she so carefully constructed within the first few hours of meeting them. Calder, on the other hand, was like a sledgehammer, smashing through her barriers with record speed and grace.

It would take a leap of faith on her part to accept his hand, blindly trusting him not to hurt her—one that she wasn't sure she was capable of making. Her mind told her to stop, that he would end up being just like all the other losers she'd dated in the past, while her intuition asked her what the hell she was waiting for and reminded her with every breath that Calder was different from any man she'd ever met.

That was exactly what scared the shit out of her.

She could see herself easily falling head over heels for the man who stood before her, offering something no normal man could—a life filled with uncertainty and adventures she'd never know as a human. Her conversation with Gerri replayed in her mind: *"Shifters are much different from humans when they first meet their mate. They know immediately that she's the woman they've waited their entire life for. The entirety of their world changes with one scent."*

"What does that mean?" she'd asked Gerri.

"Oh, sweet girl." Gerri had smiled at her. *"Think of it this way. When a shifter male finds his mate, his life is no longer about just him. His life becomes about loving and protecting his mate, knowing that she is safe, well loved, and happy."*

"That sounds pretty fantastic. Do these relationships tend to last long?" Daisy had asked.

"Forever. There are very few divorces in the shifter world."

But it was the last thing that Gerri had said to her that stuck in her mind more than anything else: *"Does having a mate who is one hundred percent committed to you sound like such a bad thing? Is it bad to know that your mate will never speak unkindly to you or stray? Think of how free the love between mates can be when there is an absolute and unwavering commitment."*

Before she said yes or no to his question, she had to know one thing. "Am I your mate?"

She watched as he sucked in a deep breath, his amber eyes glowing as he spoke. "Yes."

All she had to do was take his hand.

Gerri's words replayed again in her mind. *"Does unconditional love sound like such a bad thing?"* Daisy drew in a deep breath and stood, placing her hand in his. "Don't make me regret this."

"Never."

Eleven

Daisy's question had shaken Calder. He'd had no idea that Gerri had explained what it meant to be mated to a shifter, but clearly she had and Daisy knew exactly what his outstretched hand meant.

His blood heated nearly to the boiling point when she placed her tiny hand in his. His heart beat hard and fast in his chest.

"She's accepting us!" his wolf said in awe.

Calder wasn't about to spend time wondering how Gerri had found his mate, or why Daisy, a mere human, so easily accepted him despite knowing very little about him or his species. He pulled her close, her chest brushing against his. A low growl bubbled up from his throat as his lips closed over hers, unable to wait another second to see if she tasted as sweet as she looked.

As he deepened the kiss, he was rewarded with a husky feminine purr that sounded just like that of a feisty little kitten. Her fingers tunneled through his hair as he nipped at her bottom lip, gently sucking it into his mouth.

With each new moan he drew from her mouth, he learned that his mate's passion flowed deep in her veins. The scorching heat she threw off burned him like none other ever had. Scooping her up, off her feet and into his arms, he carried her as fast as he could to the bedroom.

"Are you sure this is what you want?" he asked as he set her gently on the four-poster bed.

***

"Make love to me, Calder." For once in her life, Daisy knew exactly what she wanted—and there would be no going back. This wasn't like her former relationships, where she'd waited, hoping it would be worth it in the long run. It never had been. Each new relationship that she'd slowly worked herself into had been a complete disaster, and look where those relationships had ended up: endless screaming matches and broken promises.

This one would be different. She was done taking her time and praying for the best. She was going to jump in and take the plunge. No holding back. This time she would tell her lover exactly what she wanted and how she wanted it.

Gone were the ridiculous nighties she'd hid her curves beneath, in the hopes of looking more appealing to the man she was with. If she was to be Calder's mate, he would have to accept her for who she was, curves and all—and by the hungry look on his face, it didn't look like her curves were going to be a problem for him. Not in the least.

Her body shook, but not from fear. Oh no— anticipation tore through her, and the thought of his warm touch in her most intimate places left her trembling with desire. He was on her a second later, his hands roaming everywhere at once as he kissed a trail from her ear down her neck. The sensual onslaught was almost more than she could bear, and she wondered if it was possible to climax with minimal stimulation.

The sound of her t-shirt being torn from her body should have startled her, but it didn't—in fact, heat pooled in her belly at the savage action. A breathy moan flew from her mouth when she felt the heat from Calder's mouth circling her nipples, and they peaked instantly.

"I can't wait to taste every inch of you, Ást," he groaned.

She had no idea what 'Ást' meant or what language he had spoken; she'd have to remember to ask him later. For now, all she could focus on was his hand cupping her sex.

Lost to the throes of passion and need, Daisy could do no more than claw at Calder like the wild beast she'd suddenly become. She almost came on the spot when he yanked her yoga pants from her legs, followed by the silky white panties that hid beneath.

"This is what I've wanted since the second I saw you in the bathtub."

She had expected him to roll up his sleeves and dive right in, so to speak. Instead he took his time, making good on his promise of tasting every inch of her with long hot strokes of his tongue up and down her thighs, gentle nibbles on her calves, and finally kissing each of her polished toes before sucking them gently into his mouth.

Good God, the foreplay alone would be her downfall. Never had so much attention been lavished upon her at one time. It made her head spin.

Her back arched off the bed and she tossed her head from side to side as his tongue landed on her clit, sucking it gently into his mouth. He repeated the motion until her entire body shook and she cried for more. He slid one figure deep inside her, then another, rocking them back and forth, paying special attention to the area just behind her clit, an area she'd had no idea existed until he'd begun massaging it.

Brilliant white lights flashed all around her as she felt her body explode into a million tiny pieces. She briefly wondered if they'd ever find their way back to her to leave her in one piece as she was before, or if she would remain a slew of broken floating pieces, all because one climax with Calder had blindsided her, slamming into her and knocking her into a neighboring universe.

"You taste like the sweetest of candy." Calder's voice was thick with lust, and his eyes glowed with a hunger so raw and wild, she begged for more.

A closer look at his full lips revealed a pair of, honest to god, fangs that had partially descended. Unsure if she should be worried or not, she gave him a questioning look as he covered every inch of her body with his.

"I promise only a few nibbles, until I mark and claim you as my mate."

Daisy didn't know why, but those words sent a shiver through her spine. Feeling the head of his cock pressed against her entrance, she decided to push the thought away to a later time.

Calder nipped playfully at her lips. When she gasped in surprise, he took full advantage and plunged deep into her mouth. Hot and hungry for more, his kiss was one for which she had no comparison, filled with desire and lust. More than a kiss, it was a seduction on the highest level, a promise of what was yet to come.

"Tell me you want me, Ást. I need to hear the words."

"Fuck me, Calder," she said on a whisper, staring deep into his glowing amber eyes.

"Ah, that's it, Ást." He thrust deep inside in one swift move, swallowing the guttural moan that flew from her mouth.

He was larger than she expected, far larger than anyone she'd previously been with, stretching her almost to the point of pain. Calder held perfectly still for several moments, giving her body the time she needed to adjust. He stretched her arms above her head, covering them with his. Hand in hand he kissed her slowly, making love to her mouth.

Only when the pain subsided, turning instead to the feeling of fullness, and she started to rock her hips against him did he move. He didn't pull out and plunge right back into her, no—he circled his hips pushing deeper inside of her than she would have thought possible. His slow sensual strokes turned to long, lazy thrusts, slowly letting her climax build with each move he made.

Twelve

Calder pulled back from the kiss as he pushed his cock deeper into his mate, staring deep into her chocolate brown eyes, lost to the lust scorching a trail through his body. *Mine!* The mating call raged deep within, demanding that he skip marking her and go straight to the claiming. And he would. Before the night was through, she would be his. Forever.

In the meantime he was bound and determined to claim her from the inside out so she would know that only he could bring her the pleasure she desired. Each moan he drew from her spurred him on, shifting positions as he found her favorites and sent her flying to the stars with more climaxes than he could count.

He'd nearly lost the struggle with his self-control countless times, as her pussy clamped down on his cock, trying to milk his seed from him, but he held on each time, needing to make sure his mate was fully satisfied.

***

Daisy'd had no idea sex could be so raw, and sweet at the same time. Calder had given her countless orgasms—his stamina was off the charts—but that last one would be forever branded into her mind. She reached up to her neck, her fingers sweeping gently over the spot where he'd bitten her—"claiming her," as he'd later called it.

He had waited until the moment just before she was sucked under by another orgasm. He'd shouted, *"Mine!"* before she felt his fangs pierce the soft spot of her neck, just above the shoulder.

The stinging pain she'd expected never came. Instead, every nerve ending in her body sprang to life, consuming her every thought. Raw emotions, his and hers, flooded her mind as he continued to pound his cock in and out of her, relentlessly, never slowing.

She felt the same rush of cold air that she'd felt in the kitchen just before he had shifted into wolf form, and saw the same swirl of majik surround them, making her feel as if she were undergoing some sort of fundamental change.

Her gums had itched. She remembered reaching up to touch her mouth, shocked to find that her canines had descended. A whisper in the wind brushed softly against her ear, telling her to claim her mate, and she did. With her newfound fangs, she bit down on his neck in the exact spot he had bitten her. His blood poured over her tongue and down her throat, setting off a frenzy she was helpless to stop.

Their fangs disengaged at the same time. He licked the mark once then twice, sending shivers through her body, and she followed suit. A guttural growl rose from his throat as he picked up his pace, and she could do nothing more than hold on tight for one hell of a ride.

She swore the pounding he'd given her pussy was one for the Guinness Book of Fucking World Records, literally. They had to have a category for that, right?

Even as she lay there glowing in the aftermath of sex, wrapped in his arms, she had a hard time believing all that had happened in such a short amount of time. She reached up to see if her canines were still as long as she remembered, or had she imagined the whole thing.

A soft sweep of her fingers over the spot she'd bitten him confirmed that it did indeed really happen.

"Careful, Ást. You'll wake the beast once again, and you'll not get a lick of sleep tonight."

"Really? How is that even possible?" She knew, better than most, how the human body worked.

"The operative word here is 'human'—, Ást."

Her eyes widened in surprise. "Did I say that out loud?"

Calder chuckled. "I can hear and see your thoughts now, as you can and hear and see mine. All you have to do is listen and look closely."

"No! Seriously?" Daisy closed her eyes and pictured a big juicy burger, loaded with bacon, lettuce, tomatoes, pickles, onions—the works.

Calder groaned. "Now you're just being mean, Ást. Rest. I'll make you a bacon burger for breakfast if you want."

"Holy—you really *can* see my thoughts! I have to see if it works for me too. Think of something, quick!"

"As you wish."

Daisy cleared her mind, concentrating on her mate—and as strange it sounded to her, that's what he was. Within seconds, images of her bent over the side of the bed, him pushing into her from behind, appeared in her mind. "Ohhh, I like where you're going with this." She continued to watch until her core once again flooded with heat.

In a flash, Calder vaulted from the bed and pulled her to the edge by her ankles, positioning her exactly how he wanted her. With her feet flat on the floor and her ass in the air, he slammed deep inside of her wetness. "I can smell your desire, and feel how desperately you want my cock back in your pussy."

"Yes!" Daisy shouted, grabbing on to the sheets for support.

Calder wrapped his hand around her hair and gave it a slight tug, arching her back and lifting her chest from the bed. He wrapped his other arm around her waist and pulled her close. His mouth closing over the mating mark he'd given her earlier.

Within minutes Daisy was once again soaring through the heavens, shattering into those familiar tiny pieces. However, this time, she noticed something different. Her bond with Calder pulled her scattered pieces back together, forming a version of herself that was stronger and more resilient than she could have ever imagined.

Thirteen

Daisy awoke to the shrieking sound of Calder's cellphone blaring through the room. She flew to a sitting position, and flipped on the bedside light, knowing any call that came in at three in the morning would be bad.

"What happened?" Calder said as he answered the call.

Whatever it was, it wasn't good. The tone of Calder's voice coupled with the sound of sirens squawking off in the distance confirmed what she already knew. Years' worth of training in the ER kicked in immediately and she dashed from the bed to grab the first set of clothes she could find.

Much to her dismay, Calder's words were not the ones she expected to hear.

"You should stay here, Ást. Until I know it's safe for you."

She turned to face him, annoyed by the very idea that he wanted to control her. The first thought that popped into her mind, flew from her mouth. "What does that mean? Ást?" It was a silly question, she knew from the moment she'd spoken it. It was hardly the time or place for this discussion, all circumstances considered.

He paused for a minute then slid on his jeans. She watched as he pulled a T-shirt over his head. "It means 'love' in Old Norse."

Well, didn't he know just how to melt her heart? "Aw, that's so sweet. But I'm going with you."

Calder shook his head. "No." His voice was firm and unwavering.

"Yes." Daisy had her own demands if she was going to be his mate. "I'm a trained and capable ER doctor. What if someone needs medical attention?" She wasn't backing down. No way in hell.

"Ást, please—just until I know what the situation is," Calder begged.

Hands on her hips, Daisy flew into a rant. She decided she needed to put her foot down and nip that shit in the bud right now. "You need to listen up, buddy. I agreed to take a leap of faith and come out here to see if I was your mate. And I am, but that does not give you the right to tell me what I can and can't do. Especially when we're talking about possibly saving lives. Now *you* need to take that leap, and trust that I know what I'm doing. I can take care of myself. I always have."

Looking far less happy about it than she had hoped, he inclined his head and agreed to her demands. "Fine. We're leaving in two minutes. Grab a jacket—it's cold out."

She met him by the front door in one, with her jacket and medical bag in her hand. She'd learned long ago to take it everywhere she went, never knowing when an emergency might pop up.

The drive to town was quicker than she had expected. Calder filled her in on the way—there was a fire at an older apartment complex. They weren't sure that everyone had made it out safely, and that didn't sit well with him. The thought of losing one of his packmates hung heavy in his mind.

Not that he had voiced a single word of his concerns. She'd felt them all through their new mating connection. At first, Daisy had sensed the strong emotions pouring through her. Due to the nature of the situation, she'd held a degree of worry for anyone that might be trapped in the building, but knew the strong sense of angst and worry that damn near buried her had come from her mate.

***

Calder threw the vehicle in park and jumped out, rushing to where Alex stood anxiously watching the blaze. The few fireman they had on the scene battled the fire with all their might, but the flames would not be deterred.

"What do we know?" Calder asked the chief.

"My nose tells me that someone's been up to no good, that's what."

"Is everyone out of the building?" Calder paced back and forth, waiting for an answer.

"We're not sure. Whatever accelerant was used to start the blaze is messing with our ability to detect any scents at all."

"Fuck." Calder jammed his fingers into his hair.

"It's not good, boss," the chief stated plainly.

"How many are unaccounted for?"

"One woman and one child."

"Jesus. Has anyone been able to get in there?" Calder had to get in there to check things out. If members of his pack were stuck in an inferno he had to try everything in his power to get them out.

"Boss, I know what you're thinking, but it's too dangerous. Even with our advanced healing, the flames are too hot. We've been concentrating our efforts on one spot hoping to cool it enough for someone to get in there and have a quick look-see, but we're not having much luck."

"Has anyone asked for reinforcements from neighboring towns?"

"Griffin had banned any outside contact."

"As of this moment the ban is lifted. If we need outside help until we get our services to the level we need them, then so be it."

"On it, boss." The chief grabbed his cellphone from his pocket and called local dispatch for assistance.

"Is there anything I can do to help?" Daisy placed a comforting hand on his lower back. Having her provided more support than he would have guessed when he'd first argued about her staying back at the house. He'd never admit it out loud, but he was glad to have her standing next to him even if there wasn't a damn thing either of them could do. He reached down and twined his fingers with hers.

Fourteen

"**W**ho's the big-ass bitch?"

Embarrassment poured through Daisy. Her cheeks burned from the blush that she knew covered them. Calder dropped her hand, quickly spinning on his heel ready to take action, knowing the chief would keep an eye on the fire and update him should the need arise.

"What the fuck did you say?"

Daisy gasped when he grabbed the weaselish looking man by his throat and lifted him off his feet to make direct eye contact. She should have felt sorry for the man when Calder slammed him up against the concrete building, but she didn't. Not even a little bit.

Instead, an unfamiliar feeling swept through her. She tried to catalogue it, but couldn't. Her heart swelled at the sight of her mate defending her honor. No one had *ever* done that for her.

"What did you say about my mate?" Calder's voice was thick with anger as his fangs descended, a clear warning to all who surrounded him.

Daisy watched as his face elongated, while his body remained human. It was the weirdest thing she'd ever seen.

Calder dropped the choking, sputtering man to the ground, hard. Majik, thick in the air, swirled around her mate's body, but this time Daisy had no problem seeing through the misty haze.

"You will answer your Alpha."

Daisy's skin itched as Calder issued the command, thick with majik. The air around her felt charged with a power so surreal she panted for air. She looked around to see if the others nearby had also succumbed to the effects of the powerful majik.

Her head spun and bewilderment coursed through her as she looked around. The people who moments ago had surrounded her were gone, replaced instead by wolves—including the man who had been on the ground.

Daisy's tongue felt unusually thick when she tried to speak, and the itching she'd felt earlier in her gums had returned. Her stomach twisted as the hair on the back of her neck stood on end. A brief flash of nausea passed over her and almost sent her sprawling on her ass. In the back of her mind, a large brown wolf charged her, fast and furious. Daisy opened her mouth to scream, but nothing came out.

The wolf crashed into her body, knocking her to the ground.

"We are one," the animal growled in her thoughts.

The ground quaked beneath her knees. She tried to stand, damn near passing out when she looked down at her feet and saw soft, fuzzy paws where her beautiful toes should have been.

"Calder, what's happening?" Daisy cried in her mind, though all she heard was the sound of a wolf howling.

"Calm yourself, child. The Alpha speaks." A strange feminine voice invaded her mind.

"Let it be known to all that Daisy is my mate as decreed by the Fates. For all those who question the legality of our mating, look to her now. See that she is one of us, bound forevermore to me. Those who have the audacity to insult the Alpha's mate will pay dearly. I am Alpha of Twisted Tail and there are several who would do well to remember that."

Calder's voice boomed in her head, and though they'd spent hours in conversation and more hours making love, the voice in which he had spoken surprised her. It wasn't his normal voice, the voice she'd become familiar with. He sounded like her mate, yet at the same time he didn't. Curiously, she was the only one who kept her head held high and straight ahead, watching her mate. The others seemed as if they struggled to remain upright.

"Listen to the power in his voice, child. He is the true Alpha of this pack. Those who questioned him are now feeling the power of a true Alpha, some for the first time in their lives."

"Who are you?" Through her conversations with Calder, she knew he often spoke to his wolf. Was the voice in her mind her wolf? It was either the wolf or she'd lost her mind. Maybe the stew she'd made was bad and making her hallucinate?

"I am you and we are one, child. Breathe free; all is well with your mind. I will guide you in our majikal and ancient ways—ways that your human body and mind have no inkling of."

Daisy did as her wolf instructed and sucked in a deep breath, not feeling threatened by the voice, nor intimidated by it. The voice comforted her, cocooning her in her favorite blanket, keeping her mind peaceful—and quite frankly, keeping her from losing it altogether.

"What do we do now?" Daisy asked her wolf, having no idea what the proper protocol was.

"We wait."

***

Calder sensed Daisy's shift the moment it had started. Surprise, shock, amazement—any of those words could have worked for the emotions that zinged through him at the knowledge that his mate had been gifted with a wolf of her own. Odin had indeed found her a worthy mate for him, and had rewarded her in kind.

The worry he'd felt when he first realized that his mate was a human vanished. Anyone who sought to challenge her position would first go through him and his wrath, and a pretty sight it would not be.

He continued to press his power on the pack as a whole. From this moment forward, he was done with the games, done with the holdovers from the corrupt former Alpha. His mate would be safe, protected; it was non-negotiable. Those who longed for a different life were welcome to leave.

The sound of incoming sirens howled in the distance. Calder eased up on his display of raw power, his features returning to normal from his half shift. The pack recovered quickly from his emotional outburst aimed at defending his mate's honor, and shifted back to human form. His sweet Daisy was the last wolf standing. He approached, reveling in the beauty of her animal—thick chocolate brown fur that matched her eyes. His wolf panted and whined his approval.

He remembered her fear: *"Don't you ever worry about getting stuck in animal form?"* He reached out, stroking her fur. *"Feels good, doesn't it, Ást?"*

She whined, leaning in to rub her head against his leg.

"All you have to do to shift back is imagine your human form. Let the transformation come naturally."

Fifteen

Thankfully back on two legs, Daisy stood next to Calder as a contingent of fire trucks from neighboring towns rolled to a stop. She was amazed at how much her life had changed in less than twenty-four hours. Not only had she mated a shifter, much to her surprise, she'd become one herself. Talk about some crazy-ass shit! She was a little miffed that neither Gerri nor Calder had given her a heads-up to the possibility that she could end up sprouting fur and a tail, an issue she'd take up with both of them later. Her questions would wait until she was certain all pack members were safe and accounted for.

The sound of howling pulled Daisy from her thoughts. Before she could process what was happening, Calder's head snapped toward the sound. He took off in a blur—only to come to a dead stop, falling to his knees.

Daisy screamed in horror as she watched her mate collapse, blood pouring from the fresh hole in his chest. Two men she didn't know tackled the man who had insulted her. A gun fell from his grip and bounced on the ground.

She ran to Calder's side, assessing his injury. *"Can he recover from this?"* she shouted in her mind to her wolf.

"Not without intervention. He's losing too much blood."

"Can you help him?" the fire chief asked.

"Yes, but I need my bag. It's on the front seat of his truck," Daisy said, as she ripped the thin T-shirt from Calder's body.

"Once the silver bullet is removed, he'll start to heal."

"Silver bullet? Who would use such a thing?" Daisy asked in dismay.

"Someone who wanted the Alpha dead. It would be the fastest way to kill him."

"Fuck!" The sight of the wound was bad, deep and messy, not something any doctor liked to see.

Daisy had no idea if Calder could hear her or not as he lay on the street, but she had to try reaching him. *"Hang on, Calder. Just a little bit longer and I'll be able to get this bullet out of you. My wolf said you could heal, once it's gone."*

"Here's your bag, doc." The chief dropped her bag at her feet.

"Thanks. What's your name, chief?" Daisy glanced up at the man. If she was going to be the Alpha's mate, she needed to start learning a few names.

"Jared Jacobson Engle."

He pronounced Engle in an odd fashion. The g languidly rolling off of his tongue suggesting his name had some special connotation. As the newcomer she had no idea why his name would be a big deal.

"Daisy, run!" Calder shouted in her head.

"Surrender to me, now," her wolf demanded, snarling in her mind.

Catching a glimpse of the discarded gun out of the corner of her eye, Daisy closed her eyes and listened to her wolf, her intuition telling her the animal would do everything in its power to protect her and their mate.

The wolf didn't hesitate, not for a second. A bat of an eyelash and a bystander would have missed her ferociousness as the wolf lunged for Jared's throat, tearing the fleshy chunk of meat from his body and dropping it on the ground.

The man reached for his neck, and gurgling sounds accompanied the sprays of blood that coated her fur. Her wolf—certain that he had no chance for recovery, and that he no longer posed a threat—relinquished her control and Daisy shifted back to her human form.

"Calder!" Daisy dug through her bag as quickly as possible. She'd already wasted too much time in the few seconds it had taken her wolf to deal with the threat.

Finding the case she needed, she spread it out on the ground and grabbed her scalpel. She sliced a small line over the area where the bullet had lodged in Calder's chest, all the while speaking to him in a calming voice. "I almost have it. Just stay with me another minute and I'll have that silver out of you."

Working diligently she separated the skin, then carefully reached in with a pair of tweezers to grab the edge of the silver bullet. She prayed removing the bullet would do the trick and allow his healing to kick in. She had no idea how shifters healed or anything about the majik that flowed through their bodies. She could only go by what her wolf had told her, and she had to trust that the animal knew what she was talking about.

"There we go." The bullet slid free from Calder's chest, and she dropped it on the ground.

"Will he be all right, doc?"

For the first time, Daisy looked up, almost horrified by the number of people surrounding her, watching her every move.

Calder coughed and his eyes slowly flickered open. "Daisy." He tried to yell, but only managed a faint whisper.

"Shhh. I'm here." She glanced down at the wound, only to see the skin beginning to knit itself back together.

"Yeah," Daisy said with a smile. "He'll be just fine."

Whispers from different people standing around reached her ears. "Did you see how she saved our Alpha?"

"Dude, she took down Jared in two seconds flat."

Daisy should have been horrified by the conversations about her and the brutality of her actions, but she wasn't. The man would have killed her and taken away any chance she had at saving Calder. If she had to do it all over again, she couldn't say that she would have done things any differently.

Sixteen

Daisy stretched, muscles aching that she'd had no idea even existed. She didn't know what time it was, and didn't really care. The night before had been filled with twists and turns that she had never expected to face in her life.

"Good morning, Ást." Calder yanked her from her thoughts by initiating a hot trail of sensual kisses over her shoulder and back, followed by lazy licks with his hot tongue, tasting every inch of her. His hand cupped her breast and gently massaged.

"Good morning, indeed. How are you feeling?" Still worried about his injury from the night before, Daisy moved to roll over and face her mate.

"I'm fine, thanks to your quick thinking." Calder held her firmly in place, his hand tight on her hips. He slid the length of his cock against her backside, teasing her.

Daisy giggled, wiggling her ass against his cock. "I just did my job."

"From what I heard last night, it was far more than your job." Calder nibbled on her mating mark. "I think I should show you just how grateful I am for saving me."

"Oh *really*."

"Mmmhmm."

Daisy gasped as Calder flipped her on her back and pulled her legs apart in one swift motion. Her fingers flew into his hair as his mouth came down over her, gently sucking her clit into his mouth.

"I don't think I'll ever get tired of seeing you go down on me. It's so fucking sexy." Daisy had propped herself up on her elbows and was watching Calder's every move.

"Good, because I can't imagine ever tiring of your taste. Now, lie back and relax so I can thank you properly."

She decided against arguing, knowing her reward would be immense. And ohh boy, was it ever, as he licked her slit furiously, his tongue dipping in and out of her pussy. Her legs quivered with each shift of his pace. She wrapped her legs around his neck as he slid two fingers inside her wetness, driving them in and out. She was surprised by the knowledge that he'd held back the first time they'd made love.

Within minutes, Daisy found herself flying off toward the heavens, screaming his name as her climax slammed into her. Calder was on her the next second, his cock pushing against her, demanding entrance.

"I love watching you come," he said as he slammed home.

His Twisted Tail

Epilogue

A week later

Daisy had indeed taken a leap of faith in becoming Calder's mate, and she knew deep in her heart it was a decision that she would never regret. The love that Gerri had described, that Daisy had never imagined, filled every moment of her new life with Calder. He was everything Gerri had described and more.

> *Attentive—check.*
> *Caring—check.*
> *A fabulous lover—check.*
> *Kind—check.*
> *Possessive in all the right ways—check.*

He worshipped each and every curve on her body in and out of the bedroom, never making her feel self-conscious like the men from her past. As for the whole love part of the equation—well, as silly as it had sounded to her the first time the thought had popped into her head, yeah—she loved her sexy shifter and she had no problem telling him each and every day.

As for her job, she'd emailed her boss, giving her notice that she was quitting, another non-regret. The hours sucked and the stress was high.

Twisted Tail had a serious shortage of medical staff, and with her mate's help and resources she was looking forward to building and staffing her very own clinic—a dream she had never thought possible.

She had planned on taking a day trip back to her small apartment to pack up the things she wanted with her at Twisted Tail and donate the rest to charity, but Calder had insisted on hiring movers to pack everything up for her and deliver it to her new home. It was a plan she could live with—the hassle of moving was definitely not her forte, and she was most happy to avoid any and all parts of it.

There was only one thing she had left to do, and that was to pen a short letter as a thank-you to the woman who'd believed her when no one else had, and who had made her new life possible. Daisy grabbed a pen and paper and sat down at the table to scribble out her thoughts.

Dear Gerri,

Thank you for letting me run into you that day on the street. My life is now better than I could've ever imagined, all thanks to you.

Sending all my love,
Daisy

ABOUT THE AUTHOR

New York Times & USA Today Bestselling Author Melanie James is the author of more than two dozen books. She grew up in western Pennsylvania before heading off to Chicago, seeking new adventures. She found life in a big city fun for a while and even met the love of her life there. Melanie quickly tired of the hustle and bustle of the concrete jungle and settled down with her one true love in northeast Wisconsin.

Melanie has two kids, three step-kids, a beautiful daughter in-law, and the cutest grandbaby. She also has two dogs and two cats that often make appearances in her books.

She loves to hear from her readers and fans. You can connect with her online:
http://www.authormelaniejames.com
http://www.facebook.com/AuthorMelanieJames

Sign up for her newsletter to get all the latest information about new releases and sales. You will also be registered for the monthly giveaway! You could be her next winner!

http://www.authormelaniejames.com/newsletter.html

If you enjoyed reading ***His Twisted Tail***, she'd be eternally grateful if you'd let the world know!

Review it.

Tell other readers why you liked the book, or any of her books, by leaving a review on Amazon, Goodreads, or your blogs. Reviews are of the utmost importance when it comes to distributors and retailers. They also help new readers make informed decisions when selecting a new book or author.

Recommend it.

You can help others find this book by recommending it! It's easy. Just tell them! Seriously! Social media is a great platform to spread the word in reader groups and discussion boards. If you love the books or leave a review, feel free to let her know at melanie@authormelaniejames.com so she can thank you with a personal email. Your support means more than you'll ever know! Thank you!

Read more from Melanie James

Black Paw Pack
Fur Ever Yours

The Fates etched Rafe & Mina's destiny in stone long ago. Now, one twisted wolf seeks to destroy them both. Will he succeed or will Mina and Rafe's bond be strong enough to survive?

The legends and sagas of the Norse tell tales of mystic warriors, the Berserkers. Heroes with hearts so fierce, loyal and courageous the Gods endowed them with a supernatural gift—the spirit of the wolf. As the time of the Gods faded into the shadows of yesterday, the wolf warriors held fast to their old ways, becoming outlaws in their ancestral lands.

In a new age, in a new land, the packs rebuilt their lives faithful to their sacred ways. In the pack of Black Paw, one man stands above all others, Rafe Erikson. His unquestioned authority and skill have fulfilled all but one part of his destiny, to find his mate. What happens when he learns that his destined mate is bound to the twisted leader of a rival pack?

In the saga of Black Paw, there can be only one choice: To follow your destiny at any cost.

A Hot Piece of Sass

Tanner Larsen isn't your ordinary wolf shifter. He's more. Believing he's been cursed by the Gods, he's all but given up on finding his one true mate. When he catches the sweet strawberry scent of his Fated female, worlds collide and ancient legends are revealed. Tanner discovers that his curse may be the only way to save his mate when a rogue wolf tries to destroy the lover's destiny.

Twice the Sass –

Cursed by the Fates at birth, Tad and Taavi Olsen have until their twenty-fifth birthday to find the one true mate they must share for an eternity. With the deadline hanging over their heads, they finally catch the scent of their fated mate. Will she accept them in time to save their lives, or will they prove to be too hot for one curvy female to handle.

Fur Ever Witched

Erin was tired of hiding her true nature. Bound by the secrets of her heritage, she found herself stuck between a rock and a hard wolf. When her secrets are unveiled all hell breaks loose.

Lucas Jansen's plan for life was simple: Serve his pack, find a mate, and start a family. Now that Lucas has found his mate the next step was claiming her. Or so he thought. Everything he believed is about to be turned upside down as ancient legends and a forbidden love push him toward a path of self-destruction.

His mate was everything he had ever wanted, and everything he had vowed to destroy. Will Erin be his curse or salvation?

You Bet Your Sass

After losing a bet with Taavi Olsen, Lars Jakobsen finds himself on stage for a weekend doing something he never thought he'd do: Stripping for the ladies at one of Blue Creek's most infamous establishments, The Horny Wolf.

When the unmistakable sweet scent of his mate nearly knocks him on his ass, all bets are off. Or are they?

Sofia Martinez wants a one-night stand, but Lars wants more. Will she keep him chasing his own tail? Or will they get their happily ever after?

Watch Your Sass

Polly Reynolds had sworn off the thought of ever finding a mate. She was perfectly content living out her life as a single lady with all the freedom to do what she wanted, when she wanted. Everything was going according to plan until a group of vicious rogues set their sights on her. Can she survive what they have planned for her?

Down in the dumps and with no real plan to move forward, Emmett Klein finds himself in an unfamiliar position when his Alpha sends him to Blue Creek to help defend the local pack from rogue attacks. Will Emmett snap out of his slump to help those in need, or will it be too late?

Books by Melanie James

Twisted Tail Pack

His Twisted Tail

Bearly Twisted

Her Twisted Heart

Twisted Desires

Black Paw Pack

Fur Ever Yours

Fur Ever Witched

Fur Ever Wicked

Black Pa Wolves

A Hot Piece of Sass

Twice the Sass

You Bet Your Sass

Watch Your Sass

Literal Leigh Romance Diaries

Accidental Leigh

Serious Leigh

Hopeful Leigh

Haunting Leigh

Joyful Leigh

Disastrous Leigh

Tales from the Paranormal Plantation
Gertie's Paranormal Plantation
Back to the Fuchsia
When You Witch Upon a Star
Hex U

Karma Inc. Files
Karma Inc.
Mission Impawsible: A Karma Inc. Novella
Shame of Clones

Éveiller Drive
Ava & Will
Kara & Dave
Laura & Alan
Jamie & Brad
Ashley & Jeff
Valerie & Greg

Stand Alones
Conjuring Darkness
Snowflakes, Exes & Ohs

Riverton Romance
A Valentine's Surprise
A Deadly Obsession